# ATTICUS MAXIMUS

## BOTTOMUS BURPS OF BRITANNIA

For Jackus Farticus who lives in Britannia.    F. A.

Scholastic Children's Books
A division of Scholastic Ltd
Euston House, 24 Eversholt Street
London, NW1 1DB, UK
Registered office: Westfield Road, Southam, Warwickshire, CV47 0RA
SCHOLASTIC and associated logos are trademarks and/
or registered trademarks of Scholastic Inc.

First published in Australia by Scholastic Australia, 2010
This edition published in the UK by Scholastic Ltd, 2012

Text and illustrations copyright © Felice Arena, 2010
The right of Felice Arena to be identified as the author
of this work has been asserted by him.

ISBN 978 1407 12905 1

A CIP catalogue record for this book
is available from the British Library.

Printed in the UK by CPI Bookmarque, Croydon, CR0 4YY
Papers used by Scholastic Children's Books are made
from wood grown in sustainable forests.

1 3 5 7 9 10 8 6 4 2

www.scholastic.co.uk/zone

# FARTICUS MAXIMUS

## BOTTOMUS BURPS OF BRITANNIA

### AND OTHER
### FOUL-SMELLING STORIES!

#### WRITTEN & ILLUSTRATED BY
#### FELICE ARENA

SCHOLASTIC

# CONTENTS

## CHAPTERUS ONE

# I'M FARTICUS

On a quiet Tuesday in the ancient city of Rome, sometime in the late afternoon, two mothers stood at a window watching their sons play on the cobbled street below.

'What are those boys up to now?' scoffed Bettius, one of the mothers. 'Why can't boys play nicely?'

'Bettius,' shrugged Jennius, the other mother. 'You

should know by now. Boys will be boys.'

'But look what my Rex is doing to your poorus little Antonius!'

Bettius stuck her head out of the window.

'Rex, that's **enough roughus play**! Get off Antonius! Get your bottomus away from his face, now!' she yelled.

'I can't, Mum!' Rex shouted back to his mother. 'We're in the middle of a battle. I'm the greatest and smelliest gladiator of all time, Farticus Maximus, and Antonius is his arch enemy, the stinky gladiator from Britannia, Gassius Brutus.'

Rex blew a wet raspberry into his forearm.

**BBBRRRRPPPPPPPPPPPPPPPPP!!!!!!**

'Take that, you barbarian!' he yelled to Antonius, who was pinned under his bottomus. 'Feel the strength of my potent windus!'

# BBBRRRRPPPPPPPPPPPPPPPP!!!!!!

'Rex! Don't you make me come down there!' Bettius hollered. 'Get off Gassius... I mean, Antonius, now!'

'Bettius, don't worry,' sighed Jennius. 'Antonius can fend for himself. It's his favourite game at the momentus. It seems that every boy in Rome is playing this game – pretending to be Farticus Maximus versus Gassius Brutus. So let them be.'

A knock came at the door.

'Oh, this must be my sister, Dora,' Bettius exclaimed, moving away from the window. 'She said she was going to drop in with a new friend of hers who's visiting from Egypt!'

When Bettius opened the door she gasped, as did Jennius. Dora's friend was not what they were expecting. She was the ugliest woman they had ever seen. She had a big, black, bushy monobrow, a large, crooked nose, and a **hairy mole** on her chin.

'Stop staring,' whispered Dora to Bettius. 'She's new in town and doesn't have any friends.'

'I can see why,' quipped Bettius. 'And I thought the Egyptians were a pretty bunch!'

Dora introduced Petra to Bettius and Jennius. After a few minutes of small talk and cups of pomegranate juice, the topic came back around to Rex and Antonius.

'Well, you might be right, Jennius. Looks as if Antonius is getting my boy back,' said Bettius as she and the other women moved to the window.

Antonius now had *his* bottomus firmly pressed down on Rex's face.

**'Eat my windus, Farticus Maximus!'** he shouted.

'Good for you!' Jennius cheered her son.

'Ewwww!' squealed Rex. 'That's GROSSIUS! MUUUUMMMM! Antonius just did a *real* fart in my mouth!'

'That serves you right. I told you not to play roughus!' Bettius replied. 'That's what you get when you pretend to be Farticus Maximus!'

'Who's Farticus Maximus?' asked Petra, who up until now hadn't said much.

'You don't know?' croaked Jennius. 'Aside from Emperor Bullius, he's one of the most famous Romans around!'

Bettius, Jennius and Dora proceeded to tell Petra all about the great Farticus Maximus.

Who's
Farticus Maximus?

# CHAPTERUS TWO

# A SECRETUS

'So, let me get this straight,' said Petra. 'When he was a boy, he was called Barticus, but everyone called him *Farticus* because he had a **major gas problem**. His windus was so smelly and powerful no one could live near him – except for his mother, Helena, with the help of orange-scented handkerchiefs...'

'They're called *snotus-rags*,' Dora informed Petra.

'Um, yes, *snotus-rags*,' Petra repeated. 'And his mother would wear a snotus-rag to block out her son's **hideous stench**.'

The other women nodded. Petra went on. 'And it was around this time that Farticus realized he could use his **powerful windus** as a weapon. Later he was discovered by Sinus, an old man with no sense of smell, who convinced Farticus to become a gladiator. With his dangerous gas he'd blow his opponents away.

He would literally kill them with his windus...'

'Um, we don't say "kill" in Rome. We say "**butterfly-kiss**". We don't want to upset the kids,' interrupted Bettius. 'And we say "**hug**" instead of "stab". Again, the kids.'

We say 'BUTTERFLY-KISS', not 'kill'.

And 'HUG' for 'stab'.

'Got it,' sighed Petra. 'So, where was I? Sinus became Farticus's manager...'

'Oh, and don't forget Sinus's beautiful daughter Rhina, who, luckily, also had no sense of smell. Farticus and Rhina fell in love!' added Jennius.

'Right,' said Petra. 'So, Farticus then became the **greatest gladiator of all time**. When he was rich enough, he retired, bought a big villa, adopted three sons, Rotteneggus, Odorus, and Stinkius – children who also had farting problems – and lived happily ever after with Rhina, his mother and Sinus.'

Petra let out a huge sigh.

'Yes, but there's more,' said Bettius, taking over. 'Another gladiator, who was also known for letting them rippus, appeared on the scene. His name was Gassius Brutus. He was the greatest and smelliest gladiator from Britannia. He came back to Rome to avenge his brother's death. Farticus had killed, I mean, **butterfly-kissed** Black Dog Brutus in one of his gladiatorial battles.'

'But here's the best part,' said Dora, jumping in. 'Farticus didn't want to fight Gassius to his death. That is until he discovered that his true love Rhina had once been Gassius's girlfriend. So, to prove his love for her, Farticus agreed to fight him. How juicy is that?'

'Yes, but then Emperor Bullius got word of the fight,' said Bettius, once again taking charge of the conversation. 'Bullius thought that this would make for a great event – the stink-off battle of the century! He thought it would boost numbers at the Colosseum, the grandest stadium in the world, and make him look good. So, Bullius ordered Farticus to fight Gassius. But our **wicked** Emperor had a plan. He didn't want just one of them to win. He wanted to see them both dead.'

Bettius raised her eyebrows as if to say, 'Wasn't that shocking?' and then continued...

'Fortunately, Farticus and Gassius worked this out mid-battle and decided to team up and break away from the **bloody clutches** of our Emperor. The two of them, together with Farticus's family, fled Rome and have never been seen since. That was six months ago and Emperor Bullius still has seven legions of his army out searching for them. He is sure to **hug** each of them when they are captured. So there, I hope that explains it for you.'

'Um, yes. It's more than I was expecting,' answered Petra. 'So, where do you think Gassius, Farticus and his family are hiding? Surely they must be hiding in Britannia? That's where Gassius is from, no?'

'Yes, that's what everyone in Rome thinks,' nodded Jennius. 'But Britannia is a large place. It's wild, cold and damp, and its towns and cities are full of **dirty thugs** and **barbarians**. It's not a nice place at all, so I've heard. Who knows if they'll ever find them up there?'

**'Cough! Cough!'**

Everyone turned to see Bettius. She had a funny expression on her face . . . and coughed again.

'What? What's on your mind, Sis?' asked Dora.

'Can you all keep a secretus?' Bettius responded. The other women nodded.

'And Petra?'

'Of course she can,' snapped Dora. 'She's from Egypt. She doesn't know anyone here. Except for yours truly,

whom she randomly befriended while I was picking out lamb heads at the market. Who would she tell anyway?'

'OK,' inhaled Bettius, leaning in conspiratorially. 'My neighbour told me that her best friend's son, Cornelius, helped Farticus and Gassius get out of the city that day they **escaped from Bullius**. He told her that they were indeed heading to Britannia, and would be staying at Gassius's **secret hideaway** ...'

Bettius lowered her voice. The others inched in closer.

'... in a farmhouse just outside of the Britannian town of Aquae-Sulis.'

# CHAPTERUS THREE

# BULLIUS

In his very, very, very big palace, Emperor Bullius lounged on a number of large pillows, as two slaves massaged his feet.

'Excuse me, oh Great One,' said Emperor Bullius's favourite general, General Yesmanus, 'but I think one of the spies you sent out to mingle with the citizens has learned something to do with the whereabouts of Farticus and Gassius.'

'Well, I certainly hope so,' grumbled Bullius, gesturing for his slaves to leave the room. 'The last two came back with absolutely no informationus at all – nothing, zippus, zilchus! So I had to **feed them to the lions**. I hope this one doesn't have the same bloodius fate. Although ... I do love watching my big, adorable pussycats dine on **human flesh**. Send him in.'

When the spy strolled into the room, Emperor Bullius gasped. It was the **ugliest** woman he had ever seen.

'State your name, grotesque one,' announced Bullius, trying not to stare at the woman's large, crooked nose and her big, bushy monobrow.

'My name is Martius,' said the woman, taking off a wig. 'And I am not a woman, but as you can see, your Greatness, I am a man. Disguised as a woman, I'm

known to the locals as Petra.'

'Well, how very **sneaky** of you,' snorted Bullius. 'Well, speak up – what news do you have of Farticus and Gassius? Do you know where they are?'

'Yes, I do. They are in Britannia,' said Petra-who-was-really-Martius, proudly.

'We already know that!' huffed Bullius. 'Feed him to the lions!'

'No!' shouted Petra-who-was-really-Martius. 'They are hiding in a farmhouse just outside the town of Aquae-Sulis.'

Emperor Bullius turned to his general.

'Aquae-Sulis?'

'Yes, Aquae-Sulis, oh, Great One,' General Yesmanus replied, pulling out a map for Bullius to see. 'It's west of

Farticus is hiding here (Aquae Sulis, Britannia).

We are here (Rome).

Londinium. See. It's here. You know, it's the town with all the public baths.'

'Ah, yes, **Aquae-Sulis**. I don't know why they just don't call it Warm Waters or Bubbly Springs . . . or something as simple as Bath. It would be easier for me to remember. I can't be expected to know every bleedingus town in the empire.'

'Um, excuse me, Great One,' coughed Petra-who-was-really-Martius. 'I was told I would be paid for giving you this important informationus. Gold, perhaps?'

'Really?' snapped Bullius. 'Paid? Your payment, dear man-who-makes-an-ugly-woman, is your honourable service to the Roman Empire. Be gone!'

'But that's **not fairus!**' cried Petra-who-was-really-Martius.

'You know what? You're right. It isn't,' smirked Bullius, stepping forward until he was only inches away from the spy's face. 'FEED HER-WHO-REALLY-IS-A-HIM TO THE LIONS!'

# NOOOOOOOOOOOO!!!!!!

Two soldiers dragged the spy, screaming and kicking, out of the room.

'So, dear Emperor,' said General Yesmanus, 'should I order our troops in Aquae-Sulis to **battle** with Farticus and Gassius?'

'No!' replied Bullius, wandering over to the window just in time to see Petra-who-was-really-Martius being thrown into a pit full of lions. 'Those **smelly gladiators** blew our troops away in Gaul on their way to Britannia a couple of months ago. They'll only do the same if we send troops to Aquae-Sulis. I have a better idea. We'll get Farticus and Gassius to come back here to Rome, where they will meet their **gruesome end.**

'But how do you intend to do that, oh Greatness?' asked General Yesmanus.

'Just you wait and see. I have a brilliantus plan,' cackled Bullius. 'Oh, look! My adorable jungle cats are playing with their food!'

'**AAAAAAAAHHHHHHH!**' echoed the chilling screams of Petra-who-was-really-Martius.

# CHAPTERUS FOUR
# NOT HAPPY

Meanwhile, in faraway cold, damp Britannia, in a run-down mud-brick hut on a dreary moor about a ten-minute horse-gallop away from downtown Aquae-Sulis, Farticus Maximus and his family had just sat down to eat their dinner.

'Doesn't this roast badgerus look delicious, boys?' asked Farticus, cutting into the tough meat. 'Once again your mother has done a fine job.'

'**More badgerus?**' moaned Odorus. 'We've had badgerus seven nights in a row!'

'Yeah,' echoed Farticus's other sons, Rotteneggus and Stinkius.

'Well, if you don't like it, don't have it!' snapped Rhina. 'It's the best I can do in this **awful, forsaken place**.'

Silence fell around the table. It was obvious that Rhina was in a bad mood.

Rhina's father, Sinus, gave her a comforting smile.

'Oh, how I do miss a good pheasant stuffed with figs, walnuts and breadcrumbs. Or even a slice of cheese with honey,' sighed Farticus's mother, Helenus Sandals.

'I'll try to hunt for something different tomorrow,' offered Gassius, chewing on his badgerus leg.

'Yes, well, for now we just have to put up with what we have here,' said Farticus. 'So please, boys, no more whining, we just have to . . .'

Suddenly Farticus broke wind, blowing out a hole in the wall behind his seat.

# BBBRRRRRRPPPPPPPP!!!!!!

His sons laughed.

'Nice one, Dad!' they chuckled, quickly reaching for their orange-scented snotus-rags.

'You call that "nice"?' grinned Gassius. 'Then take this!'

# BBBRRRRRRPPPPPPPP!!!!!!

Poor old Helena, who had been sitting closest to Gassius, had been **blown off her stool!** Everyone laughed, except for Rhina. And Helena.

'Sorry, Mrs S,' apologized Gassius, helping her up. 'Are you OK?'

'Yes, dear, I'm all right. That was a cracker! Pure and rich, a real choker! I really should've been wearing one of my snotus-rags. Not that it would've been much of a help – the orange scent has faded on most of them. Oranges, and lemons for that matter, are hard to find here in Britannia.'

'There's nothing here in bleedingus Britannia,' huffed Rhina, standing up from the table. 'Except for grey, cold windy days and dirty barbarians.'

Rhina stormed out of the hut and into the chilly night air. Farticus rushed after her.

'Rhina? What's wrong?' he asked.

'Everything's wrong, Farty!' she sobbed. 'Look what our lives have become. Hiding and living on the run in a miserable land. No contact with anyone. I hate it. **I wish we could go back!**'

'But you know that's not possible. We've just spent six months getting here – fighting Bullius's soldiers, dodging bandits, trekking over treacherous mountains and valleys. And now we're finally safe. It's going to take some time to get used to it, but you just have to give it a chance. OK? I promise things will get better.'

Farticus hugged Rhina and, once again, farted.

## BBBRRRRRRPPPPPPPP!!!!!!

And then again. . .

# BBBRRRRRRrrrrrrrr!!!!!

'Get in close. Feel that? Warm, toasty air, huh?'

'Oh, you,' Rhina grinned, playfully tapping her husband on the shoulder.

'Good. You're smiling. By the way, Gassius, your dad and I are going out for a drinkus at the local tavernus tonight.'

'What!? Again!?'

'Look, it'll just be a quick one. I'll pick up a nice goat for you on the way home. No more badgerus tomorrow! OK?'

Rhina reluctantly agreed. A few minutes later, as Gassius, Sinus and Farticus were heading out, Rotteneggus chased after them.

'Dad, I wanna come with you,' he pleaded.

'I've told you before, these drinking tavernuses are not for young boys,' Farticus said firmly.

'But I'm not a boy, I'm almost a man. And I want to be a gladiator like you someday. Please, please, let me come!'

'No!' snapped Farticus. 'Now go back inside and play with your brothers. And you'd better give up on that dream of being a gladiator. Life is different here. This isn't Rome.'

Rotteneggus grumpily trudged back into the hut and Farticus headed off to the pub with Sinus and Gassius. None of them had any idea that they were being watched from afar.

In the nearby woods something **lurked** in the shadows.

# CHAPTERUS FIVE

# PIG AND SANDAL

'Well, it looks packed tonight,' observed Gassius, as
he, Farticus and Sinus stood outside the Pig and
Sandal.

'It's always packed,' sighed Farticus, having second
thoughts and wondering if he should've stayed home

with Rhina and the kids. 'So, we do the same as the other night, right?'

'Yep,' nodded Gassius. 'We take our place at the far corner, by the biggus **open window**, so when we let rip...'

'And you will let rip,' quipped Sinus. 'You two are **farting up a storm** at the moment. Thank goodness I can't smell anything, because...'

# BBBRRRRRRPPPPPPPP!!!!!!

Farticus and Gassius farted – again.

'OK, so we have to try and hold it in, until we get to the window. We don't want to draw unnecessary attention to ourselves. We can't risk it. Someone could rush back to Bullius and tell him of our whereabouts. As far as the locals know, we're brothers. I'm a poet and you're a tiler specializing in bath tiles. And Sinus, our dad, is retired. Got it?'

'Got it!' nodded Farticus. 'But why can't I be the poet and you be the tiler?'

'Because we've been here a few times, and I've already told people I'm a poet. We've got to keep our stories straightus! Got it!? Now let's just go in, I'm thirsty!'

As Sinus went to the bar to order the drinks, the smelly gladiators weaved their way through the jostling crowd to the corner window seat.

'Phew!' sighed Farticus, while pointing his bottomus out of the window and letting rip. 'Talk about self-control. I thought I was **going to blow** any second then.'

'Me too,' sighed Gassius, also rushing to stick his bottomus out of the window.

When Sinus returned with large cups of cider, he looked flustered.

'Drink up, boys,' he said. 'I thinkus you've been recognized. See the big red-headed man at the bar? He and his friends were asking me a lot of questions.'

Farticus and Gassius glanced towards the bar and saw a large, burly man, with a mop of curly red hair, and his mates staring back at them.

Sinus whispered: 'While I was waiting for my order they were saying things like, "*Isn't there a lot of* **hot air** *in here?*" and "*This place* **stinks** *more than usual, don't you agree?*" I thinkus we should get out of here and try another tavernus.'

By the time Farticus and Gassius agreed to Sinus's suggestion, the red-headed giant of a man and his friends had already made their way over to them.

'You boys aren't from around here, are you?' the red-headed man asked in a not-so-friendly manner.

'No, we're from Rome,' replied Gassius, calmly.

'Really?' he huffed. 'You look a lot like a gladiator I used to see when I lived in Londinium years ago. His name was Gassius Brutus. He ended up **butterfly-kissing** three of my brothers – all great gladiators in their own right.'

'Yeah, well, I'm very sorry to hear about that. He sounds like a **real brute**, this Gassius Brutus,' replied Gassius. 'But I'm Markus. Markus Limericus. A poet.'

Farticus rolled his eyes, still annoyed that *he* wasn't the poet.

'Of course you are,' snarled the big red-headed man. 'Well, I'm Trevorus Pommus, but I doubt *you* are who you say you are, *Markus Limericus*.'

'Well, I can't do anything about that,' said Gassius. 'But nice chatting with you. All the best now.'

Farticus and Sinus nervously sipped their cider. But Trevorus and his friends weren't budging. They continued to stare and snarl.

'If you're a poet, recite one of your poems for me,' ordered Trevorus.

'No, no!' said Gassius. 'It's after work hours and I never compose when I'm out for a drinkus.'

'NOW!' growled Trevorus, as he and his mates stepped in closer.

'Right. Okay, then,' coughed Gassius. Farticus and

Sinus looked very worried. 'Here goes ... um ... this is one of my favourites ... um, it goes like this.'

Gassius put down his cup of cider and took in a deep breath.

> 'There once was a gladiator from Sparta,
> At all the good markets he'd barter.
> For he'd filled his bags
> With snotus-rags
> And turned out to be the best farter!'

'Now, Farticus!' he shouted. **'Let's rippus!'**

Gassius and Farticus pulled their bottomusses in from the window and let Trevorus and his friends have it.

They blew the men off their feet. Within moments the entire tavernus **erupted** into a full-out brawl. Trevorus and all the other drinkers rushed for the smelly gladiators. Sinus jumped out of the window and dashed off into the night – leaving Farticus and Gassius to fight the thugs on their own.

He was way too old to get caught up in such a riot.

Gassius and Farticus let rip, repeatedly, throwing a dozen men off their feet.

BBBRRRRRRPPPPPPPP!!!!!! POP!

POP! BBBRRRRRRPPPPPPPP!!!!!!

BBBRRRRRRPPPPPPPP!!!!!! POP!

'STOP! PLEASE, STOP! YOU'RE STINKING THE PLACE OUT WITH YOUR VILE BOTTOMUS BURPS!' pleaded the tavernus owner.

But the brawl continued until every single drinker was knocked out cold by the smelly gladiators' **deadly gas**.

'QUICK! Let's get out of here before they all recover!' shouted Farticus, stepping over bodies and rushing out the front door.

'So, what did you think of my poem? Good huh?' asked Gassius, a few steps behind.

'Don't give up on your day jobus!' croaked Farticus, sprinting down the street.

When Farticus and Gassius made it home, Sinus came running out to meet them. He was yelling and clearly upset.

'What's wrong!?' asked Farticus, seeing the alarmed look on his father-in-law's face.

'They've taken Rhina! They've taken Rhina, your mother and Rotteneggus!'

They're gone! GONE!!

'WHAT!? Who has?'
gasped Farticus.

'Emperor Bullius's soldiers
took them away!'

'How do you know it was
Bullius's men?' asked Gassius.

'Because we saw them!' replied Odorus and Stinkius
in unison, as they ran up and hugged Farticus. 'We were
playing outside when they raided the hut. They didn't
see us. We hid in a ditch and saw them take Mum,
Grandma and Rotteneggus away. We heard them say
they were taking them back to Rome.'

Farticus's heart was racing. This was terrible.

'It's a trap!' said Gassius. 'Bullius is going to use them

as bait, to catch us. We can't go back.'

'I have no choice,' sighed Farticus. 'I have to go. I have to go back to Rome and save my family.'

# 11. BUMP AND STINK IN THE NIGHT

'Here comes another one, just like the other one!' laughed Alex, as he let rip under his bed covers.

## BBBRRRRPPPPPPPPPPPPPPPP!!!!!!

'Woah, that's a ten!' snorted Reese, who was lying on a blow-up mattress on his best friend Alex's bedroom floor. 'Listen to this one!' he bragged.

There was a pause.

'There! I did it!'

'No, you didn't!' retorted Alex, listening carefully in the dark. 'I didn't hear anything. Are you sure that you... **phwoooohh! Woah, an SBD!** That's gross!'

Reese cracked up laughing. He was a pro at delivering farts of the Silent But Deadly variety.

'Not fair!' protested Alex. 'No smelly ones, just loud ones. Don't want you stinking out my room because if you ... oh, **pwhoooohh!** Another one!?!?'

Again Reese cracked up.

'Go to sleep!' Alex's dad's voice boomed from the other side of the wall.

Reese and Alex laughed quietly.

'I guess we should try to go to sleep...' sighed Alex.

'Yeah, I s'pose,' said Reese.

The two boys lay silently in the dark, attempting to doze off.

'Hey,' whispered Reese, a few minutes later. 'You awake?'

'Yeah,' said Alex.

'I'm glad your folks put back your holiday trip to next week. I had an awesome time today. Your mum and dad are cool.'

'Thanks, they are,' Alex whispered back. 'But sometimes they can be … **phwoooohh!** Did you just **let rip** again? That stinks!'

Reese snorted a half laugh.

'Sorry!' he apologized. 'I can't help it. It might have something to do with those hot dogs I ate today.'

'Well, stop it, will ya? I'm choking here. Seriously, dude, that's **foul**. Actually, it's so bad I have to open a window.'

Alex stepped over Reese and opened his bedroom window.

'There, now we can breathe,' he grunted, jumping back into bed.

'Boys!'

It was Alex's dad, popping his head into the room and switching on the bedroom light.

'Sorry, Dad, we were trying to get to sleep but …'

'It doesn't matter. I'm glad you're up. Mum called. She's having car problems. She was leaving Grandma's house when she broke down just outside of Denville. I'm going to pick her up. Will you boys be OK by yourselves? I'll only be gone an hour at the most.'

'Dad, I'm ten, almost eleven,' shrugged Alex. 'I think we can handle being on our own for an hour.'

'Well, I'll have my mobile with me just in case. And I've locked the doors and...'

'Dad, we'll be OK!' exclaimed Alex. 'You'd better go and pick up Mum. She'll be freaking out being all by herself on the side of the road.'

'Yeah, right. Okay, well, I won't be long and ... **phwoooohh** ... what's that stench?'

Alex shot Reese a dirty look. Reese winced.

'Sorry, Mr P,' he said, embarrassed. 'Um ... that was me.'

'Woah Reese, that's deadly,' joked Alex's dad. 'You could **knock out a rhino** with that! Open a window . . . oh, I see you have already. All right then, I'm off. I'll be back soon!'

'So, now what?' Reese asked Alex. 'Should we try to get to sleep again?'

'Sleep!?' Alex coughed, as he looked out the window and watched his father drive off into the night. 'You've got to be kidding? Who can sleep with your butt shooting off like it is! Let's go down to the kitchen. I think we might have some medicine for your **fart-fest!**'

Alex switched his bedroom light off and they both stomped down to the kitchen.

'Right, let's see what we've got here,' Alex mumbled to himself as he rummaged through the pantry. 'Mum gives me this fizzy drink whenever I have stomach cramps or **bad gas**. I think it's called No-Gas, Stop-Gas, or No-More-Farty-Pants or something like that. . . Ah, here it is.'

Alex tipped some of the indigestion powder into a glass of water and stirred until it became fizzy. Reese swallowed it in one large gulp.

## BBBBBUUUUURRRRRRRRP!

'Ahhhh,' he said. 'I feel better already!'

'Yeah, well, as long as it stops you from more deadly **bottom-burps**, then we're both going to be better off.'

## THUMP!

'Did you hear that?' gasped Alex.

'Yeah, I did,' said Reese. 'It sounded as if it came from upstairs?'

## CREEEEEEEAK!

'Now *that* sounded as if it was coming from outside,' said Alex, with a worried look on his face. 'Follow me.'

Alex made his way to the kitchen window, pulled back the blind and peered outside.

He gasped.

'What? What did you see?' croaked Reese.

'I thought I saw two men climbing into my bedroom window,' whispered Alex.

'What!? Are you serious?' Reese gulped. 'But your room is on the second floor!'

'They have a ladder...'

'Are they **robbers**? Are they gonna hurt us? Alex, what are we going to do?' Reese was panicking. 'Why did you leave your window open?'

Alex shot Reese a dirty look. 'Oh, right, I remember…' said Reese guiltily. 'Sorry. Darn those hot dogs!'

'Quiet!' Alex shushed Reese. 'I can hear them. They're walking around upstairs. We've gotta get out of here!'

Alex rushed to the kitchen door. It was locked. Then to the front door – that was locked also.

'My dad's locked us in,' he whispered to Reese. 'I'm going to call him. We've gotta get to the phone. It's in the lounge room. Don't say a word. We don't want them to hear us or we … **phwoooohh** … did you…?'

Reese nodded. 'Sorry, I fart when I'm scared.'

Alex shook his head and gestured for Reese to follow him.

As they tiptoed into the living room, they heard the intruders making their way down the stairs.

'They're coming down!' gulped Reese, just as Alex was about to pick up the phone. **'Hide!'**

The boys ducked behind the couch just as the two men stepped into the room. Alex cupped Reese's mouth. They both held their breath.

'Hold on, I'll check the kitchen,' said one of the men.

'All right, I'll look for the safe,' said the other.

Alex took his hand away from Reese's mouth. Together, they quietly exhaled.

'Well, no one is here...' said the voice returning from the kitchen.

'What did I tell ya, Ronnie?' said the other voice. 'They've gone on holidays. I just can't believe they left that bedroom window open. Lucky for us!'

Once again Alex rolled his eyes at Reese.

'And Griz, you're sure they have a safe in the house? Where they keep their jewels?'

'How many times do I have to tell ya? My sister works with the wife! She once told my sister that her husband, who's a jeweller, keeps some of the precious jewels at home. This home. In a safe.'

Reese pulled a face at Alex, as if to say, 'Is that true?!

Your family has a safe filled with jewels in the house?'
Alex confirmed with a nod.

'And since cracking safes open is my job, then "hello, jewels"… We just have to find the safe … and … **bingo!** Here it is! It's always behind an antique oil painting!'

Alex gasped. He peered over the couch. Yep. The robbers had indeed found his family's safe. He quickly ducked back down.

'Now, all I have to do,' said the one called Griz, 'is crack the code.'

'And you're sure you can do that?' asked the one called Ronnie.

'Yeah, of course! It looks like a three, two, five combo or a four, two … **phwoooohh!** Did you just drop one? That stinks!'

Alex shot a look at Reese. Reese shrugged. 'Sorry,' he mouthed.

'That wasn't me!' protested Ronnie. 'You sure it wasn't you!?'

'Rack off!' growled Griz. 'Now, let me be!'

Once again Alex raised himself up and peeked over the couch. He could see the burglar, Griz, turning the code combination wheel on the safe while the one called Ronnie watched intently over his shoulder.

Alex glanced at the phone. It was only a metre away from the couch. He wondered if he could get to it without the robbers seeing him. . .

'Got it yet?' asked Ronnie.

'Shut up, will ya?' snapped Griz. 'And stop **farting!** That's foul! I can't think!'

'I told ya it wasn't me!' huffed Ronnie. 'It's gotta be you! You're the one who ate that hamburger with all the onions on it!'

Alex shook his head at Reese. He cupped his hand over his mouth and nose. Reese's **smellies** were getting worse.

'Stop it!' hissed Alex. 'You're gonna blow our cover!'

'I can't help it!' Reese whispered back, as he **let loose** once again.

'Right! GET OUT!' barked Griz. 'You can't expect me to crack this safe with you **letting rip** in my face every darn second!'

'IT'S NOT ME!' growled Ronnie. 'IT'S YOU! HE WHO SMELT IT, DEALT IT!'

Ronnie shoved Griz.

'Don't push me, mate!' huffed Griz.

'Or else what?' snarled Ronnie.

'Or else I'll shove your head so far up your **butt**, you're gonna suffocate on your own gas!'

What happened next took Alex and Reese by complete surprise. The two robbers broke into an all-out brawl, right there in the middle of the lounge. As they wrestled and rolled about on the floor, Alex and Reese snuck out from behind the couch, grabbed the phone, and darted into the kitchen. The intruders were too busy fighting to notice!

Hiding in the walk-in pantry, Alex dialled his dad's mobile.

It wasn't long before the police arrived, their sirens flashing and blaring loudly. They caught the robbers red-handed just as they were making an attempt to escape by backing out of Alex's bedroom window.

'You boys were lucky you escaped without any harm,' said the officer as he interviewed Alex and Reese on the front lawn, flanked by their parents and neighbours.

'Yeah, thank goodness no one was hurt,' sighed Alex's mum, hugging her brave son tightly.

'Yes, indeed,' said the officer. 'But just one more thing ... When we got inside there was this **revolting smell** throughout the house. Do you know what that was?'

'No, officer. We have no idea!' Alex smiled, winking at his handy friend Reese.

# THE STENCH ACROSS MY SPACE

What's that stench wafting across my space?
That rotten smell drifting in my face?
I say to Hugh, we're inches apart,
'That is totally gross! Did you just fart?'

'No!' he huffs. 'No! No! No! No!
It's coming from there, it must be Joe!'
'Hey, Joe! Not cool at all,' I cry.
'You're gonna kill me – I'm going to die!'

'It's not me!' he hollers back.
'Who's that laughing? Must be Jack.'

'Get lost!' Jack barks. 'I'm not that smelly.
I bet it's a girl. It must be Nelly.'

At the back of the class is where Nell sat.
Next to Sandra, Jen, Josie and Nat.

'Hey, Nelly,' I call. 'Stop being a pain.
No more fluffies from off the chain.'


'What?!' she snaps. 'You dirty boy.
I bet you did it. That's your ploy.
Don't blame it on me, and others too.
That putrid gas came straight from you!'

'You've got it wrong. Truly,' I croak.
'It's not from me,' I stutter, I choke.
I smell it again, that revolting stink.
It's someone else. I'm certain. I think.

Then out of the blue I hear some pops.
I look up, but my jaw drops.
Could it be? The mystery farter?
Our very own teacher, Mrs Carter?

I sniff the air. Yep, she's the one.
I let everyone know. It had to be done.
'Mrs C let one rip!' I yell.
'It comes from her, that deadly smell!'

Everyone laughs, except Mrs Carter.
No one likes to be called a farter.
'Yes, I'm the one.' Her face turns red.
'Oh, please forgive me. I'd rather be dead.'

'So do us a favour,' I shout out in jest.
'No more homework,' I suggest.
'OK,' she says, 'if you button your lip.
No one must know I let one rip.'

We happily nodded with tongues in cheeks.
Yep. No more homework for two whole weeks.
A giant grin came across my face.
And gone was the stench wafting in my space.

# THE MASTER BLASTER'S VERSE

I'd like to warn you before I cut the cheese
It's going to be bad, so please, please, please

Crack a window!

Crack a window, open a door
It's gonna stink, that's for sure.

It will knock you back from here to the moon,
Beware, beware of my trouser typhoon!

That was nothing. Just a squeak.
I expected more. Not something so weak.

Beware!

Hang on. I feel it again. I really do.
Tapping at my door, door number two.

Yep. This one's for real. Deep from the core.
Horrific and nasty, that's for sure.

I don't want to alarm you, but you really must run
Because when I let rip, it'll be no fun.

My stomach's rumbling, run faster!
Far, far away from the Master Blaster.

What? Nothing? So ripped-off!
I definitely thought
I was gonna pop off.

But wait. Could it be?
This is it, just you see …

Oops!

I think I just …
um…
Could I use your toilet, please?

# THE RIGHT NOTE

There once was a girl from Jakarta,
Who sang opera, La Traviata.
She reached for a note
It came not from her throat
Turns out she's a soprano farter!

# WE ALL DO IT

Fleas do it.

Buzzing bees do it.

Mean teen queens in green jeans do it.

Let's do it, let's all break wind!

Movie stars do it.

Wild jaguars with scars do it.

Rockers with their grannies in sidecars do it.

Let's do it, let's all pass gas!


Rats and mice do it.

Even nice girls with lice do it.

Dicey dancing sailors and spice-scented tailors do it.

Let's do it, let's all fluff!

Bloggers do it.

Joggers with big dogs do it.

Giant hairy hogs in bright orange clogs do it.

Let's do it, let's all . . . phwooooh!

Bakers do it.

The LA Lakers do it.

Bad poker players, vampire slayers,

and wrinkly nay-sayers do it.

Let's do it, let's all pop off!

Physicians do it.
Phoney magicians do it.
Witches making potions and dental technicians do it.
Let's do it, let's all let rip!

Preachers do it.
Grumpy old trolls do it.
Buffed teachers wrestling deadly man-eating
creatures do it.
Let's do it, let's all do an SBD!

Yep, you do it.
I do it.
Even kings and queens, behind the scenes, do it.
Let's all do it, let's all break wind!

# IN THE JEANS

There once was a boy who loved to eat beans,

Broccoli, cabbage and other sweet greens.

The gas from down under

Bellowed like thunder

And blasted a hole right out of his jeans.

# IV. THE MOO-FART GAME

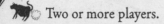

## What you will need to play this game:

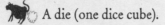 Two or more players.

A die (one dice cube).

Markers to represent each player. Note: Different coins, paper clips or bottle tops can be used as markers.

## How to play this game:

Photocopy the following six pages, and place beside each other. See diagram:

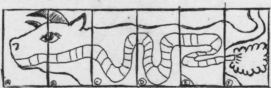

Alternatively, you can play directly from the pages in this book. Place your markers on the 'Start Here' square. Each player takes a turn to roll the die. Each player moves their marker along the spaces according to the number they have rolled. The first player who lands on the cow's gas cloud first, with the correct roll of the die, is the MOO-FART winner!

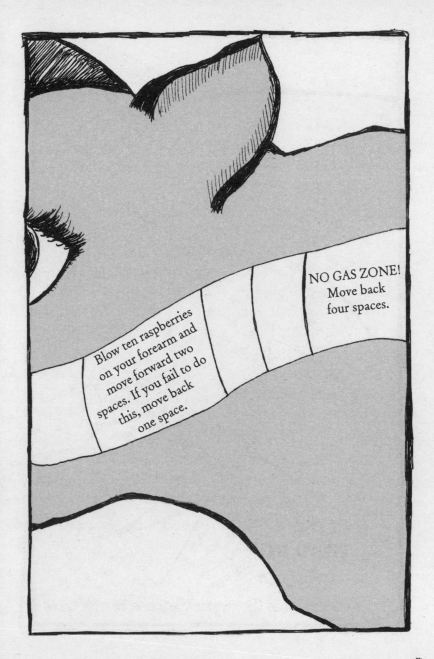

Blow ten raspberries on your forearm and move forward two spaces. If you fail to do this, move back one space.

NO GAS ZONE!
Move back
four spaces.

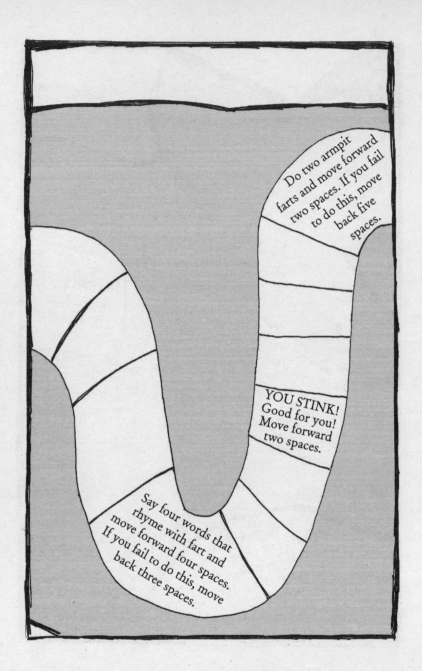

Do two armpit farts and move forward two spaces. If you fail to do this, move back five spaces.

YOU STINK! Good for you! Move forward two spaces.

Say four words that rhyme with fart and move forward four spaces. If you fail to do this, move back three spaces.

Mention three other ways to say, 'I farted!' e.g. 'I popped off!' Move forward three spaces. If you fail, move back six spaces.

TUMMY RUMBLING ZONE! Move forward one space.

NO WIND ZONE! Move back two spaces.

BACTERIA BLISS! Move forward two spaces.

In one breath, blow a raspberry that lasts for 30 seconds and move forward three spaces. If you fail, move back four spaces.

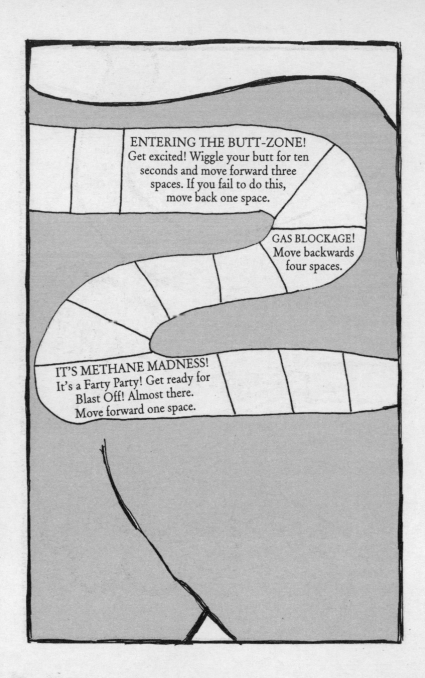

I'm Jake – president of the Three River Towns Festival Committee. I'm twelve years, two months and five days old. How did I get such an impressive title at such a young age, you ask? Well it's all because of my **big idea** – the biggest, most amazing idea ever (if I do say so myself). It all began about three weeks ago, when I headed down the street to go fishing...

I was making my way along the main street of

Waterhole, on a warm, sunny day, carrying my bucket and fishing rod.

'Hey, Jake!' cried Mr Krimble, opening up his mechanic's shop. 'Going fishing again?'

'Hi, Mr K!' I waved back. 'Yeah, you know me. Hope to catch some big ones today.'

The good thing about living in Waterhole (a small town on the banks of a large river called Queens River) is that I can fish as much as I like. I love to fish. I could fish all day, every day, and not get bored.

'I'm thinking of using my pigeons again for the festival!' enthused Mr Krimble. 'But this time I'll have them fly away from the crowds. Either that, or Mrs Smorgan suggested we could paint everyone's faces like cod – the emblem of Waterhole. What do you think?' Mr Krimble looked at me eagerly.

'Yeah, OK, I s'pose,' I shrugged awkwardly.

To be honest, I didn't think either of those ideas were good enough to get us a win, but I didn't want

to quash Mr Krimble's enthusiasm, even after the last embarrassing pigeon disaster.

Perhaps I should explain. Not too far from Waterhole is a town called Clearwater. And if you drive ten minutes further on, there's yet another town, larger than Clearwater and Waterhole put together. It's called Grand Springs. Together these three towns are called the Three River Towns.

As long as I've been alive I have never known my little town, Waterhole, to win the Three River Towns 'Town of the Year' trophy. It's a prestigious trophy which is awarded each year at the Three River Towns Festival. Clearwater or Grand Springs have always won it – but never Waterhole. And it's not from a lack of trying, believe me!

Every year, judges from a newspaper in the city of Steelburg come to the festival and wander through the streets of each town. They sample the homemade cakes and soak up the farmers'-market atmosphere. Now as far as cake stalls go, Waterhole

is up there with the best of them. But that's not
what the judges are really looking for. The trophy
is always given to the town that can entertain
the festival-goers the best. It has to be something
special. Something different and fun. Something
awesome that will blow the judges off their feet.

Last year, Grand Springs had **camel rides** at
sunset, with **glow-in-the-dark saddles** and
**Arabian belly dancers** (who were really some
of the mums from the local netball club) serving
authentic Arabian bread made in an open-fire oven.
It was pretty cool. Another year, Clearwater had
fifty **water-skiers** dressed up as famous cartoon
characters, zigzagging and doing **flips off speed-
boat ramps**. Again, very cool.

As for Waterhole, well, maybe because our town
is small and populated mostly by tired old people
whose ideas are a tad last century, we haven't been
able to come up with anything worthy of a win.
Although once we came pretty close.

Mr Krimble, the town's part-time mayor, full-time mechanic, and avid pigeon breeder, had his flock of seventy pigeons do a fly-by over the town and along the riverbank. The birds flew in perfect time to a piece of rhythmic classical music that was played through humongous stadium-sized speakers. All the festival-goers, including the judges, looked up in awe as they tapped their fingers and feet along to the beat, mouths agape, eyes wide.

Yes, it was all going so well – until it started to rain giant drops of white and brown ... the **pigeons were pooping** on everyone!

# Splat! Splat! Splat! Splat!

There was pigeon poo in mouths, on cheeks, and in eyes that had been admiring the display just a moment ago. There was **poo on everything** – even on what people were eating! Pigeon poo on fairy floss, pigeon poo on ice-cream, pigeon poo on cupcakes ... well, you get the picture. It was pretty gross. So there went our chances for winning the trophy. But as I said ... we got so close.

'Well, if you have a better idea, let me know,' added Mr Krimble. 'The committee will decide what we'll do. Today is the last day I'm taking suggestions. It would be great to have a young person's input.'

I wished I had an idea, a fresh perspective for the committee. Something tremendous to take away that slightly scary look of desperation in the mayor's eyes. But I couldn't think of a thing, not at that moment.

The idea didn't come to me until a couple of hours later when I was sitting on the bank of the river at my favourite fishing spot.

Perched on a rock just underneath a bridge that crossed the Queens River, I heard a **huge screeching** sound followed by an **enormous bang**. A truck speeding across the bridge had lost control! Before I knew it, a large aluminium container had slipped off the back of the truck,

crashed through the bridge's guardrail, and was
hurtling down towards me. I jumped for my life!

# TWOOMPP!!! CRASH!!
## SPLASH!!! SQUiSH!!!

The container passed right by me and plunged into
the muddy riverbank with an enormous **splat**.

I had launched out of the way just in the nick of
time. If I hadn't dived to the side like some World Cup
goalie, I would've been crushed to smithereens. My
fishing rod wasn't so lucky. It had been snapped in two.

After catching my breath, I slowly stepped
towards the large rust-red container as if it were an
**alien craft** that had fallen out of space. As I drew
closer I could see that the lid had popped off, and
there inside was something I never expected to see.
I thought a container like that might hold groceries,
like toilet paper or dishwashing liquid, or maybe
something fun like DVDs. But this was better, way

better than any of that. I smiled. This was so cool!

I sprinted back to Mr Krimble and told him what had happened. He then called Mr Tonkins, Waterhole's one and only policeman.

'Wow, that's some container!' gasped Mr Krimble, as we all stood there staring at it.

'Yeah. You're lucky it didn't land on you, Jake,' added Mr Tonkins, just as his mobile phone started ringing.

'Hey, Mr K, look at them all. There must be **thousands** in there!' I said, grinning and pointing at the inside of the container.

'Well, I just got word from the officers in Grand Springs, who ran a report on the truck. Turns out it was stolen from the city. No wonder it was speeding. They just found it dumped outside of Clearwater, but there's no sign of the thief. As for the cargo, they spoke to the company involved, and they said it wasn't really cost effective to retrieve them until the next truck runs through here – so it could be weeks, perhaps months, before anyone comes. In fact, it sounded as if we could do what we please with them.'

And that's when it came to me – my **brilliant idea**, the idea that was going to win us our first ever Three River Towns 'Town of the Year' trophy.

'I think you might be on to something there, Jake,' said Mr Tonkins, when I told him.

'Me too,' added Mr Krimble. 'I hate to say it, but I think it's better than using my pigeons again. So, do you want to make this your official submission to the festival committee?'

I nodded.

'Brilliant then!' smiled Mr Krimble, ruffling my hair.

Later that night, Mr Krimble dropped by my house to tell me what the committee had thought of my idea.

'**Congratulations!**' he cried, as we were sitting in the lounge room with my parents. 'Everyone loved

Jake's suggestion. Except Mrs Potts, of course. She thought it was **childish and silly**. As if *her* idea of dressing everyone's pets (and their owners) in fairy costumes and parading them through a glittering fairy castle set *wasn't* silly.'

'So, what does this mean exactly?' my mum asked, smiling with pride.

'Well, we decided I didn't have time to train the pigeons to do synchronized gymnastics to the latest Bublé hit.' Mr Krimble winked at me. 'So we're going with Jake's idea instead, and we'll use what we found in the container today. Jake said he's figured out how every single person in Waterhole can be involved.'

'What? All three thousand and sixteen of us?' gasped my father, clearly impressed.

They all looked to me.

'Yep,' I grinned. **The entire population!**

Waterhole didn't have long to get ready. There was just one week before the judges would arrive. Mr Krimble and I went to every single household in Waterhole and told them what we wanted them to do on the day of the festival.

Everyone **laughed** and **snorted** when they heard what I had planned. And luckily, most of them agreed to participate.

During that week Mr Krimble also announced that the festival committee had decided that I was to be Waterhole's official festival escort. That meant I would guide the visiting judges through the town on judging day. I was honoured to have been chosen, but it did feel like a bit of **extra pressure**, and I really hoped we would be able to pull off my big idea and impress the judges!

❀   ❀   ❀   ❀

So, the big day finally arrived. I wore my best clothes, even a tie (Mum made me wear it). I was so nervous, but excited at the same time. On the main road just outside of Grand Springs I stood with the other two official escorts, Mr Stilton from Grand Springs and Mrs Goodall from Clearwater.

Mr Stilton and Mrs Goodall **were bragging** about why *their* towns would win. They were so cocky that they hadn't even noticed me.

'Grand Springs is sure to win again. We've won it six times, you know,' boasted Mr Stilton, pursing his lips and crossing his arms.

'Well, Clearwater has won seven times!' quipped Mrs Goodall. 'And it will be number eight this year!'

'I think Waterhole has a good chance,' I interjected.

'**What?**' crowed Mrs Goodall, looking down her large beaklike nose. 'What did you say?'

'I said, I think we have a really good chance this year.'

For a moment there was no reaction from the arrogant pair. And then. . .

'Huh?' they spat in unison.

'That's hilarious! As if Waterhole could win!' guffawed Mr Stilton.

'They've never won. And they never will!' squealed Mrs Goodall, laughing loudly.

I wanted to say, 'Yeah, you just wait and see.' But I didn't. I was beginning to have doubts. Was my idea really brilliant, or was it going to be a **dud**? I didn't have a lot of time to worry about it, though, because the judges had just arrived.

There were three judges, all from Steelburg. There was Mrs Green, a plump young woman who **waddled** when she walked. Mr Banofi, a very thin tall man with **beady eyes** and greasy jet-black hair. And Ms Hartford, an elderly woman with a stone-cold expression; it looked as though her **face would crack** if she smiled.

All three had leather-bound notepads and

pencils. Mr Banofi was also carrying a large bag —
presumably with the trophy inside.

'So, where to first?' Ms Hartford asked us.

'Grand Springs, my lady,' coughed Mr Stilton,
pushing in front of us.

'Then Clearwater, dear judges,' croaked Mrs
Goodall. 'And you all know, of course, that the main
street is a car-free zone all day. So, as in previous
years, we're free to walk the streets … dear judges.'

'My lady'? 'Dear judges'? What big-time **suck-
ups**, I thought.

'Yeah, then I suppose it's us. Last. Waterhole,' I said,
as the judges and other escorts started walking off.

When we strolled into the main square of Grand
Springs, the town folk were already busily in market-
mode. Everyone was selling or buying something.
There were balloons. And hot dogs. And little kids
noisily winding their way through the crowds. Then,
out of the blue, as Mr Stilton clapped his hands,
everyone froze, even the kids.

Just then, loud music started blaring out of the enormous speakers mounted around the town square. The music was 'Do-Re-Mi' from the musical *The Sound of Music*. Within seconds everyone – yes, every citizen of Grand Springs – began dancing in time to the music. And then they even started singing along:

'Doe, a deer, a female deer. Ray, a drop of golden sun...'

I couldn't believe it. All the Grand Springs residents were dancing like **Broadway stars**. They were incredible. I looked at the judges. They were busily writing in their notepads. Mrs Green was swaying to the music. Mr Banofi was mouthing the lyrics. But there wasn't any reaction from the stone-cold Ms Hartford. It was hard to tell what she was feeling.

When the music stopped, **everyone cheered**. The judges clapped long and hard – they had obviously enjoyed it.

'I remember you mentioned last year how you loved *The Sound of Music*, Ms Hartford,' said Mr Stilton, pulling a face at Mrs Goodall and me. 'The good folk of Grand Springs have been practising that routine for the past year. I hope you enjoyed it.'

'Oh, we did!' Mrs Green gushed.

'Yes, bravo!' said Mr Banofi, still scribbling comments in his notepad.

'Right,' said Ms Hartford indifferently. 'Now, off to Clearwater.'

'Oh, yes, yes,' stuttered Mrs Goodall nervously.

I could tell that even she was impressed by Grand Springs's performance, which meant she was also worried for her own town. I had to admit, I was pretty worried too. Could we beat that?

When we arrived in Clearwater, it took no time for the residents to swing into action. Three large construction cranes had been transformed into **life-size dinosaurs**. Their necks moved up and down, and their jaws **chomped**. They moved slowly down the main street, with legs attached to the side of the cranes **stomping** noisily. Everyone gasped. And cheered. And clapped. They looked so real. It was so cool. I think it was even more impressive than the dance routine in Grand Springs. Again, the judges busily scribbled comments down in their notepads. Mrs Goodall leaned towards Mr Stilton and I and arrogantly hissed, '**Suffer, boys!** Looks as if it's Clearwater this year!'

Finally, it was Waterhole's turn to impress the judges.

When we arrived at the top of my town's main street, I nodded to Mr Tonkins, who immediately set off his police car's siren. Within ten seconds the citizens of Waterhole had all grabbed chairs and were lining up on both sides of the road.

As I gestured to the judges and the other escorts to begin moving down the street, the Waterhole townsfolk came to attention, standing like soldiers in front of their chairs.

Then it was all up to me. I raised my hand and everyone reached into their pockets and they each pulled out a **large red whoopee cushion**. Yep. Whoopee cushions. Thousands of them! All from the container that had smashed my fishing rod. There had been enough in there for every single person in Waterhole!

Moving in perfect unison, everyone blew up their whoopee cushions and placed them on their chairs at the same time. And as the judges and I strolled by, one by one, moving as if they were doing a Mexican wave, each person sat down immediately after the person beside them.

BBBRRRRRRRPPPPPPPPP!!!!!! BBBRRPPPP!!!!!!

BBBRRPPPP!!!!!! BBBRRRRRRRPPPPPPPP!!!!!!

BBBRRRRRRRPPPPPPPPP!!!!!! BBBRRPPPP!!!!!!

BBBRRPPPP!!!!!! BBBRRRRRRRPPPPPPPPP!!!!!!

Everyone started giggling and laughing louder and louder as we continued marching. I gazed over to the judges, and I could see that they were finding it difficult not to smile. I mean, seriously, who wouldn't smile at the sound of a whoopee cushion going off? But three thousand whoopee cushions, going off one after the other? Now that's entertainment!

When we reached the end of the main street and the last whoopee cushion had **popped off**, we were met by Mr Krimble, who was standing beside three empty chairs in the middle of the road. On each of those chairs were ... yep, you've guessed it, more whoopee cushions.

'Judges,' I said, pulling out a speech I had written the night before. 'I'd like to invite you to sit down on one of these chairs and experience the same **fun** that the people of Waterhole have just shared. I invite you to embrace ... (my mum helped me write this part), the **silliness** and the **simple joy** one gets from sitting on a whoopee cushion.'

'I've never seen anything so ridiculous,' huffed Mr Stilton of Grand Springs. 'Our *Sound of Music* brings joy! Not this **rubbish!**'

'Well I never!' gasped Mrs Goodall of Clearwater. 'The nerve of you to expect that these dear, wonderful, distinguished judges would ever do such a thing...'

'I'll do it!' chirped Mrs Green, quickly waddling over to the first chair. 'This will be fun!'

'That's the way!' I cheered, as the citizens of Waterhole started crowding in.

Mrs Green dropped back into the chair and...

# BBBRRRRRRPPPPPPPP!!!!!!......

Everyone cheered. Mrs Green roared laughing.

I looked to the other judges. Mr Banofi snorted at the sight of his fellow judge making a whoopee cushion **pop off**.

'Mr Banofi. You next?' I asked.

Again everyone cheered for him to take a turn.

'All right!' he said, caving in.

I caught Mrs Goodall and Mr Stilton snarling at me.

As I grinned back at them, Mr Banofi had already plonked himself down on his chair and . . .

## BBBRRRRRRPPPPPPPP!!!!!!

The crowd roared with delight. Mr Banofi broke out laughing.

'That was fun!' he giggled, like a little kid.

'Ms Hartford?' I called.

I knew this would be difficult. She was the toughest and coldest of all three judges. She hadn't smiled once today. Probably never in her entire life, I thought.

'I think I will pass, thank you very much,' she replied sternly.

The townspeople of Waterhole groaned.

'Come on, Beryl!' pressed Mr Banofi. 'Embrace the spirit of it all.'

'Yes, please, Ms Hartford,' pleaded Mrs Green.

'Oh, all right then, if you insist!'

Everyone cheered as I led Ms Hartford to the last chair.

'OK, OK!' I yelled like a ringmaster at a circus. 'I need everyone to be completely silent. After the count of three, Ms Hartford here will sit on a whoopee cushion... Are you ready, Ms Hartford?'

I waited until everyone was absolutely quiet. Ms Hartford took in a deep breath. She looked nervous. I nodded to her to get ready...

'One... two... THREE!'

# BBBRRRRPPPPPPPPPPPPPPP!!!!!!······

The crowd erupted. Everyone laughed and laughed and laughed. And no one laughed harder than Ms Hartford. She was smiling from ear to ear and I was happy to see that her face hadn't cracked.

Later that afternoon the people of Grand Springs, Clearwater and Waterhole crammed into the main square of Grand Springs, where the judges were set to announce the winner of this year's 'Town of the Year' award.

I stood nervously alongside my mum, dad, Mr Krimble and Mr Tonkins, as the judges made their way on to a large stage at the front of the crowd.

Ms Hartford approached the microphone.

'Ladies and gentlemen, thank you once again for inviting us to partake in what has become a highlight in our calendars.'

The audience cheered. Mr Krimble winked at me. I crossed my fingers. Ms Hartford continued...

'This year's performances, from all three towns, were the best yet. But there can only be **one winner**. The Three River Towns Festival is meant to be about having fun and being entertained and

I've never heard so many people **laughing so hard** at one time in my whole life, like I did today. And I've never laughed so much and enjoyed being silly so much since I was a little girl! I was literally blown away,' she added with a chuckle. 'So with that in mind, the winner of this year's Three River Towns 'Town of the Year' is . . .'

I closed my eyes.

'. . . WATERHOLE!'

'Hooray!' The citizens of Waterhole erupted in excited cheers and hugs. Somebody had even brought along an extra supply of whoopee cushions so that everyone from the other towns could have a turn sitting on one!

So, there you have it. Thanks to me and the whoopee cushions, my town won the trophy for the first time in history. It was probably the greatest day of my life . . .

What happened next, you ask?

Well, for one thing, the company that owned the

whoopee cushions turned up a few days later and we
had to give them all back. Bummer. But Mr Krimble
replaced the cod on the town's coat of arms with
a whoopee cushion! And the best thing of all, I was
made honorary president of the Three Towns
Festival committee.

Whew! Now I have to come up with another idea
for next year. Something even more explosive!

If you have any thoughts, drop me a line.

✿      ✿      ✿      ✿

# VI.

## ~~Cartoons~~ Far Cartoons

## aka famous movies with a stinky twist!

## 101 SMELLMATIANS
### (AND CRU-SMELL-HER DE VILLE)

# WHERE THE WILD THINGS FART

# THE WIND IN THE WILLOWS

**GAS**TRO BOY

## SMELLVIN AND THE CHIPMUNKS

**FART**ASTIC MR FOX

**AFARTAR**

# THE KAFARTE KID

## MR BAKED-BEAN'S HOLiDAY

## THE STINK PANTHER

**SCOOBY-POO**

## SHREK FOREVER FARTER

## CHAPTER ONE

'Wow! That's impressive, Stuart!'

Eleven-year-old Stuart Mason stepped back from his workbench, looked at his papier-mâché sculpture of a rabbit, and beamed with pride. He loved art class.

'Thanks, Miss Jones,' he said, smiling back up at his art teacher.

'You really have a talent,' Miss Jones added. 'The way

you've painted the fur. The expression on the face. It's so realistic looking. It's **truly fantastic**. Well done.'

Stuart smiled again. Miss Jones was new to his school, but already she had become one of his favourite teachers.

When Stuart got home he couldn't wait to show his masterpiece to his father.

'Dad! Dad!' he called out, running towards the voices he heard coming from the other end of the house.

As Stuart **burst** into the kitchen he stopped dead in his tracks, and almost dropped his sculpture. His father was hugging a strange woman.

# CHAPTER TWO

'Stuart!' his dad said, quickly pulling away from the woman. 'This is my friend Vera.'

'Oh, hello, I've heard so much about you,' said Vera, stepping up to Stuart and ruffling his hair. 'You're just as handsome as your dad.'

Stuart didn't say a word.

'Well, don't be rude,' his dad urged. 'Say hello!'

'Hello,' mumbled Stuart. 'Excuse me, I just have to put this down.'

Stuart left the kitchen and placed his sculpture on the table in the dining room. Just then his older sister Maggie came stomping down the stairs.

'Gotta tell you something!' said Stuart, rushing over to her. 'Did you know that Dad's got a lady friend with him, right now!? She's called Vera. What sort of name is Vera? **Sounds like a vampire's name!**'

'Yeah, I met her a few minutes ago,' shrugged Maggie, adjusting her iPod headphones. 'She seems nice. And I wouldn't be calling her a vampire in front of Dad. I think he really likes her. Are you OK with this?'

Stuart knew what his sister meant by that. Their mother had died two years ago and for a long time Stuart didn't like the idea of his father seeing other women – ever. As far as he was concerned, no one was going to replace his mum.

Well, that's what he had thought up until now . . . Stuart knew that no one could ever truly replace his mother, but he was beginning to think that maybe he should just want his dad to be happy.

'Yeah, I'm OK with it,' admitted Stuart. 'Do you think she makes him happy?'

Maggie nodded.

'All right, you two,' called Mr Mason, entering the dining room. 'I'm going to get some takeaway Chinese food. Vera will be having dinner with us tonight, so I want you to make her feel welcome. Understood?'

Stuart and his sister nodded.

'So, kiddo, I'd like you to go in there and get to know her ... OK? Can you do that for me?'

Stuart reluctantly agreed and shuffled back into the kitchen.

# CHAPTER THREE

'That sculpture you were carrying when you came in looked very interesting,' Vera said, as Stuart stepped back into the kitchen.

'Thanks. I was going to make a dog but then decided to make it into a rabbit instead, so...'

Stuart realized something. Where was his dog, Charlie? He usually ran up to greet Stuart the moment he got home from school.

'Something wrong?' asked Vera, picking up a glass of wine.

'Yeah... I'm just wondering where my dog Charlie is.'

'Oh, I told your dad to put him outside,' explained Vera, taking a sip from her glass.

'Why?' asked Stuart. 'Did he need to pee?'

'No,' replied Vera. 'I don't think animals should be inside. **Especially smelly ones**.'

Stuart couldn't believe this woman. Who did she think she was?

'But Charlie always stays inside with us. And he's not smelly.'

'I beg to differ,' Vera coughed.

'I'm going to get him…'

As Stuart moved to go outside, Vera stepped directly in front of him, blocking the door.

'I said, smelly animals belong outside. You got it? If I lived here, I'd make sure that dog **never** stepped inside again,' she snarled.

'She *is* a vampire,' thought Stuart to himself. He couldn't believe his dad liked her.

Stuart brushed past Vera and went outside.

'Well, I'll stay outside *with* him then,' Stuart called back crossly, even though he was actually a little bit scared of her.

# CHAPTER FOUR

Half an hour later, when the Chinese food containers were spread out on the dining table and Maggie and Vera were seated, Stuart's dad asked him to come inside.

Stuart came in to join them – with Charlie trotting just a few steps behind him.

'Um, darling, Petey, look…' Vera said, placing her hand on Stuart's dad's arm and pointing at the dog.

Stuart quickly blurted: 'Dad, you know that Charlie always sits at my feet while I eat. **You can't suddenly kick him out!**'

Mr Mason looked at Vera, then at Stuart.

'All right, he can stay, but don't feed him from the table, OK?'

Stuart caught Vera glaring at him. She obviously wasn't happy.

As everyone dug into dinner, a **potent, rotten smell** began to waft across the table. Vera was the first to complain.

'Oh, that's **disgusting!**' she exclaimed, grabbing her napkin and holding it to her nose.

'Woah, that is **rotten**,' agreed Stuart. 'Maggie just **let one rip!**'

'Get lost! It wasn't me, you dweeb!' Maggie snapped.

'You sure?' asked Stuart. 'Because that was a real **SBD–Silent But Deadly!**'

'Now, that's enough, you two,' warned Mr Mason. 'If either of you needs to leave the table and visit the bathroom, I suggest you go now.'

'But it wasn't me!' responded Stuart and Maggie in unison.

'As much as I love dogs, I'm sorry to say I think it was your beautiful Charlie,' said Vera.

'It wasn't Charlie!' protested Stuart, who knew very well that Vera's remark about loving dogs was a lie. 'That definitely smelled like a **human fart**. Charlie's **fluffies** smell more lemony!'

'Stuart! Don't be crass!' huffed his father.

A few minutes later, the **rotten, smelly stench had returned**.

'Oh, there it is again!' gasped Vera. 'Oh, Charlie, you cheeky little thing!'

'Stuart – take the dog out NOW!' ordered his dad.

'But it wasn't Charlie!' Stuart protested again. 'I'm sitting closest to him. And it doesn't smell...'

'NOW!'

# CHAPTER FIVE

Later that night Stuart was chatting to his sister in her bedroom.

'I don't like her. I don't know what Dad sees in her,' he complained. 'And I don't like how she calls Dad "Petey" and not Peter.'

'I knew you weren't ready for Dad to see someone else and you're still thinking of Mum and...'

'No! No! It's not that,' exclaimed Stuart. 'It's because she doesn't like animals. She doesn't like dogs. She doesn't like Charlie. Dad can't be with someone who hates dogs!'

'Oh, it looked to me as if she liked Charlie. I don't think she *hates* dogs,' said Maggie.

Stuart told his sister what Vera had said to him in the kitchen. He was certain that if Vera lived with them she would make sure Charlie wouldn't be allowed inside. Ever.

'And you know what?' added Stuart. 'I bet she's the one who **farted at the dinner table** tonight.'

'Don't be gross!' winced Maggie, flipping through a magazine.

'No, I'm serious! It wasn't me and you said it wasn't you...'

'And it wasn't!' reiterated Maggie.

'Yeah, so that leaves Dad and Vera,' said Stuart. 'And Dad wouldn't have because he was on his best behaviour, and...'

'You're nuts! You know that!?' scoffed Maggie. 'Just forget about it, will ya?'

'No way! I can't forget about it. If only I can prove that she...'

'She what? Farted! Then what? Dad's not going to stop liking her just because she **broke wind**. Everyone does, you know?'

'I know ... but if I can prove that she hates Charlie and animals, then Dad might have second

thoughts about her because he loves animals and. . .
That's it!'

'What's it?' asked Maggie.

Stuart didn't tell his sister what he had in mind.
But he had just thought of a daring plan.

❁    ❁    ❁    ❁

# CHAPTER SiX

The following night, the Masons and Vera were all seated around the dining table again. Stuart's dad had made a roast.

'Wow, Dad, that looks fantastic!' praised Maggie.

'Yes, Petey, this is absolutely superb,' raved Vera.

Stuart rolled his eyes.

'Thanks.' Stuart's dad grinned. 'Well, everyone, dig in! Stuart, what's wrong with Charlie?'

Charlie was curled up in his basket in the corner of the hallway, outside the dining room, sound asleep.

'I don't think he's feeling well, Dad, or maybe he's just tired,' said Stuart. 'He'll be OK.'

'Maybe he needs to go outside and get some fresh air,' added Vera.

Stuart shot Maggie a look as if to say, 'See, I told you if she could have her way she'd have Charlie outside for ever'.

As everyone was enjoying their meal, a potent,

disgusting stench filled the dining room.

'Oh, goodness! What a **putrid smell!**' gasped
Vera. 'I think Charlie *is* sick. That's not pleasant at all.'

'It's not Charlie!' said Stuart.

'How can you be so sure?' asked Vera. 'It's quite
disgusting. Don't get me wrong. I love cute little
Charlie, but what he just did is quite revolting.'

'Take him outside, Stuart,' his father coughed.

'But it wasn't him, Dad. I know it! And it wasn't
me. And it wasn't Maggie...'

'No way!' Maggie squealed.

'And it wasn't you, Dad, was it?'

'Of course not!' croaked Mr Mason.

'Then **it was her!**' said Stuart, pointing at Vera.

🌸      🌸      🌸      🌸

# CHAPTER SEVEN

'How dare you! Well, I never...' Vera huffed. 'I'm sure it was the dog. **Ladies do not make awful smells**. It most certainly was your dog over there!'

'Stuart!' growled his father. 'You apologize at once to Vera and take Charlie outside.'

'I will, but before I do...'

Stuart got out of his chair and made his way to Charlie. He then picked the dog up, brought it over to the table and dropped it beside his plate. Everyone gasped. It wasn't Charlie. It wasn't even a real dog. It was a papier-mâché sculpture, a masterful replica of Charlie that Stuart had made at school that day.

'It couldn't have been Charlie. The *real* Charlie is in my bedroom. **Vera let rip the SBD** and she was probably the one who farted last night, too!'

Stuart smiled. He was proud that his plan had worked. He felt as if he was one of those TV detectives solving a mystery.

'Why, I have never been so **humiliated** in my entire life,' cried Vera, rising from her chair.

'Stuart, how could you?' said his father, raising his voice. 'You apologize to Vera at once!'

'I'm sorry,' stuttered Stuart, noticing the disappointed look on his father's face. 'But she said that if she lived here she wouldn't allow Charlie to stay inside. She hates Charlie. She hates dogs, can't you see...?

'That's enough!' roared Stuart's dad. 'You apologize to Vera, now!'

'It's too late for apologies, Petey... I'm leaving!' Vera threw her napkin on to the table and **stormed out the front door**. Stuart's dad chased after her.

❀　　❀　　❀　　❀

# CHAPTER EIGHT

Stuart thought he would've felt happy about exposing Vera as the **dinner-table farter** and **dog-hater**, but he didn't. When he saw his dad moping after he came back in without Vera, Stuart felt awful.

'I'm sorry, Dad, I didn't mean to. . .'

'Goodnight, Stuart.' Stuart's father cut him off as he made his way upstairs to his bedroom.

Stuart now **felt worse than awful**.

Later that night, he tapped on his father's bedroom door and shuffled in.

His father was lying on the bed reading a book.

'Dad,' Stuart said softly as he approached, 'I really am sorry. I hope you don't hate me.'

'I don't hate you,' he replied, looking up from the page. 'But no one likes to be embarrassed like that, son.'

'I know. I hope Vera will forgive me. I was just

afraid she was going to kick Charlie out of the house. And Mum really loved Charlie, and...'

'Hey,' said his father stopping him. 'It's OK, I knew that Vera didn't like Charlie, or, well, any dogs, or animals in general.'

'You did?'

'Yeah. It was obvious. But that didn't mean I couldn't like her.'

'I'm sorry,' Stuart said again. 'Maybe we can have dinner with Vera at a restaurant or...'

'No, I won't be seeing Vera again. We decided to go our separate ways. Probably for the best.'

Mr Mason rolled over and Stuart didn't know what else to say. He looked at the picture of his mum on his dad's bedside table and felt like the worst son ever.

# CHAPTER NiNE

*DING DONG!*

The doorbell sounded early the following morning. Charlie skidded across the hallway floor to the front door, barking his head off.

'Good morning?' greeted Mr Mason as he opened the door and saw a woman smiling on the doorstep.

'Good morning,' she smiled. 'You must be Stuart's dad. I'm Miss Jones, Stuart's art teacher. I've seen you a couple of times at the school.'

'Yes, of course, I remember,' said Mr Mason, suddenly looking a bit **shy**.

'Miss Jones!?' cried Stuart, coming down the stairs and catching sight of his art teacher in the doorway.

'Hi, Stuart,' she called out. 'You left your watch in the art room yesterday. You took it off while you were working on that **papier-mâché dog**. I thought you might need it during the school holidays.'

Miss Jones handed Stuart's watch to him.

'Well, that's very kind of you, Miss Jones,' said Stuart's dad.

'Oh, it was nothing at all, Mr Mason. And please, call me Holly.'

'OK, Holly, only if you call me Peter.'

Stuart caught his father and Miss Jones making **goofy smiles** at each other.

'And who's this adorable boy?' Miss Jones added, crouching down to pat Charlie.

'That's Charlie!' said Stuart.

'Well, thank you again, Miss ... I mean, Holly,' said Mr Mason. 'I have to head to the hardware store and...'

'Um, this is a little awkward,' began Miss Jones, standing back up. 'I have to confess. I didn't just come here to drop off Stuart's watch ... oh, gee, I've never done this before...'

Miss Jones took in a deep breath.

'Um, Peter ... I was wondering, if you're up for it, would you like to go out for coffee or lunch sometime?'

Stuart gulped. Did his art teacher just ask his father on a date? Cool!

Mr Mason smiled.

'Well. . .' Mr Mason began to say, and just then Stuart **smelled something rotten**. He shot a look over at his father and Miss Jones. By the expressions on their faces it was obvious they could smell the **stinky stench** as well. **Someone had just let rip.**

# CHAPTER TEN

Stuart knew he hadn't popped off, and by the shocked look on his father's face it seemed clear it wasn't him either. And . . . it didn't smell like one of **Charlie's lemony fluffs**. Which meant it had to have been Miss Jones! An **SBD** from his art teacher?

Stuart had to think quickly. This was his chance to make up for ruining his father's evening last night with Vera.

'Woah!' he gasped. 'Sorry about that, Miss Jones. Charlie is a bit **windy** this morning! Must be the new dog food I gave him earlier.'

There – Stuart had done it. He had put the blame on Charlie!

'Oh no, it wasn't cute little Charlie,' said Miss Jones, blushing deeply. 'I am so sorry, and more than a little embarrassed. But it was me. I've been **gassy** all morning. I don't know what it is . . . must have been something I ate. Peter, Stuart . . . please forgive me. This is so awkward.'

Stuart couldn't believe it. Miss Jones had confessed when she could easily have **let Charlie take the rap**. 'What a legend!' he thought. He liked her now more than ever. And apparently so did his dad. . .

'Not awkward at all,' Mr Mason shrugged. 'I had the same problem a couple of days ago. We're only human. And, by the way, yes!'

'And, yes?' squeaked Miss Jones.

'Yes. I would very much like to go out for lunch with you some time. Say tomorrow around noon?'

Miss Jones smiled. Mr Mason smiled. Stuart smiled.

This was turning out to be the best day ever.
Just then the **rotten smell returned**.

'Now, that wasn't me! I swear!' winced Miss Jones.

'And it wasn't me,' Stuart and his dad echoed in unison.

They all turned to look at Charlie.

'**It was Charlie!**' cried Stuart excitedly. 'I can smell lemon!'

Everyone laughed. And this time they were all very happy to be able to blame the dog.

# VIII.

# Fart-tunes

## aka famous songs with a stinky twist!

## ACHY BREAKY **FART**

## MY **FART** WiLL GO ON

**YOUNG FARTS RUN FREE**

## WiND BENEATH MY WiNGS

OOPS i FARTED AGAiN

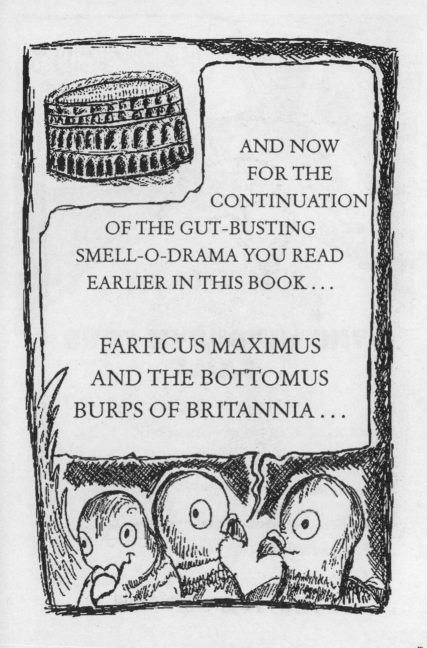

AND NOW
FOR THE
CONTINUATION
OF THE GUT-BUSTING
SMELL-O-DRAMA YOU READ
EARLIER IN THIS BOOK...

FARTICUS MAXIMUS
AND THE BOTTOMUS
BURPS OF BRITANNIA...

IX.
**FARTICUS MAXIMUS:**
BOTTOMUS BURPS
OF BRITANNIA
PART 2

## CHAPTERUS SIX

# THE WINDUS IN YOUR SAILS

Tossed about in an old wooden sailboat a couple of kilometres out to sea, with the white cliffs of Britannia fading in the mist, Farticus and Gassius slowly made their way to the mainland, the first leg of their journey back to Rome.

'Thanks again for coming along,' said Farticus, as he struggled to adjust the sail.

'No, problemus,' said Gassius. 'I couldn't let you fight Bullius and his men by yourself. We have to save Rhina, your mother and Rotteneggus. End of story. But you know this will be the **battle of all battles**. We'll be walking right into Bullius's trap.'

'Yeah, I know,' sighed Farticus. 'But we've blown his troops away before and we will **blow them away again**. I hope Sinus and the boys will be OK back in Britannia. I couldn't risk putting them in danger by this trip. Hey, why have we stopped?'

and Gassius gazed at the sea around them
realized that their sailboat had come to a standstill.
It was just bobbing up and down in the calm water like
a cork.

'The windus has gone. We just have to wait until it
picks up again,' shrugged Gassius.

'Yeah, right, not if I have any say in it. I can't afford
to wait around. Rhina needs me!' said Farticus. 'Get up
and let's get this thing moving! Let's **unleash our own
windus**. Remember, we are the kings of wind!'

Farticus jumped to his feet and pointed his bottomus
in the direction of the sail – and let rip. Not missing a
beat, Gassius joined in, and within moments the sailboat
was skimming through the water at an incredible speed.

'**There we blowus!**' cried Gassius, with a huge grin
plastered across his face.

'You can say that again!' smiled Farticus. 'Keep going!
We'll reach land in no time at all!'

# BBBRRRRRRRRPPPPPPPP!!!!!!

# POP! BBBRRRRRPPPPP!!!!!! POP!
# BBBRRRRRRRPPPPPPPP!!!!!!

The sailboat was now whooshing along, and as if to congratulate the gladiators, a pod of dolphins bobbed up out of the water and rode along joyously in the boat's wake. That is, until they got a whiff of the smelly gladiators' wind. One dolphin suddenly did a **back flip** and darted off in the opposite direction for dear life, but the rest of his friends stopped dead in the water and rolled over on to their backs, **like stunned mullets**.

'OK, I think we have to take a break, my bottomus can't take this any longer,' puffed Gassius, after two hours of continuous wind-making.

'Fair enoughus,' agreed Farticus, also **exhausted by the constant popping off**. He couldn't remember the last time he had farted so many times in a row. It was definitely a personal record. 'Luckily, it looks as if the "real" windus is picking up.'

In fact, the wind had picked up considerably – bringing along with it mountains of dark, thunderous clouds. The calm sea was whipped up into enormous choppy swells.

'I don't like the look of this,' gulped Farticus. 'Hold on, Gassius. I think we're in for a bumpy ride!'

And within minutes, Farticus and Gassius found themselves in the middle of a humongous storm. The waves now soared to **twenty metres high**, tossing the sailboat about like a discarded snotus-rag in one of Rome's gushing fountains.

'HOLD ON!' yelled Farticus, as wave after wave came crashing down on him and Gassius.

'I AM!' Gassius shouted back, coughing and spluttering. 'FARTICUS! I'VE NEVER BEEN

SCARED OF ANYTHING IN MY LIFE. BUT I'M
TERRIFIED RIGHT NOW! I CAN'T SWIM!'

'JUST DON'T LET GO! WE'LL BE OK!'

Just then the top half of the boat's mainmast
snapped off, bringing the sail down with it as it crashed
on to the deck.

'LOOK OUT!' cried Farticus, just as the mast
descended and knocked Gassius overboard.

'NO! GASSIUS!' screamed Farticus.

Farticus caught a glimpse of Gassius bobbing amidst the crashing waves, just before he was engulfed by the wild swell.

Tears welled in Farticus's eyes as he slumped to the deck of the sailboat, desperately clutching to what was left of the mast.

His friend was gone.

# CHAPTERUS SEVEN

# PRISONERS

Back in Rome, in a very, very, big palace, Helena, Rhina and Rotteneggus were being closely watched by Emperor Bullius's armed guards.

But unlike most prisoners who are locked away in **dark, damp dungeons**, Farticus's family was being guarded in the Emperor's very own luxurious lounging room, sprawling on pillows and selecting delicious, exotic fruit from platters held by slaves. There was even a lap pool.

'Oh, no thanks,' Helena waved a servant away. 'I've eaten way too much, I'm busting. Excuse me! Yes, you. Attend to my feet!'

Farticus's mother ordered one of the Emperor's servants to begin massaging her feet, as she lay back on her bed of fluffy pillows.

'I can't believe you!' scoffed Rhina with her arms

crossed. 'Your son is probably **risking his life** at this very momentus to make it back to Rome to save us and you're here living the high life.'

'Yes, I suppose you're right,' huffed Helena, gesturing for the servant to stop. 'But, I really think you should lighten up. Enjoy this while you can.'

'How can I enjoy this?' snapped Rhina. 'That evil Bullius has ripped our family apart. Taken us as prisoners, using us as bait, no doubt, so he can catch and then ultimately **butterfly-kiss** my beloved Farticus – your son!'

'OK, OK, enough of making me feel guilty,' pouted

Helena. 'It's just that after living in Britannia, it's nice to have a bit of comfort. Come on, admit it. This is nice.'

Rhina screwed up her face and turned away from Helena.

'Even Rotteneggus is loving this!' Helena added. 'Look! He's taken a real shine to the Emperor.'

Rhina turned to see Rotteneggus playing with Emperor Bullius. They were having a pretend fight with wooden daggers.

'You're very quickus, my dearus boy!' smiled Bullius. 'A

real **gladiator in the making**! Perhaps even a future general in my army!'

'You really think so?' gasped Rotteneggus, his eyes twinkling with excitement. 'Because my dad said I shouldn't even think of being a gladiator. He thinks it's not the life for me.'

'Well, that sounds unfair to me. Your father is a selfish man,' the Emperor snarled. 'Because you have a real talent. If you were my son, I'd definitely want you to be a **great fighting warrior**.'

Rotteneggus smiled again, before Rhina ordered him to sit beside her. She was uncomfortable with her son getting so close to the evil Emperor. Bullius looked in her direction with a slimy smile on his face and called for his right-hand man, General Yesmanus.

'Yes, oh Great One,' Yesmanus said, sidling up to the Emperor as quickly as he could.

'Any updates on Farticus?' Bullius whispered, continuing to smile at Rhina, Helena and Rotteneggus through clenched teeth.

'Yes. We just got wordus that he was spotted north of the city. Blew away thirty of our men, three farmers, and a herd of sheep. It won't be long before he is here.'

'Good. My plan is coming together. And the medicine man from Britannia, is he here yet?' asked Bullius, as he moved towards the open-air window and looked down at his beloved lions.

'You mean the Druid? The one who claims he has a special flower plant that when eaten **stops one from farting** for several hours? Yes. He just arrived.'

'Brilliantus,' cackled Bullius. 'Now all we have to do is wait for Farticus to show up.'

# CHAPTERUS EiGHT

# DRUID

Farticus ducked in and out of the dark laneways of Rome like a rat scurrying from garbage pile to garbage pile.

He was in a panic about being seen. He had made it this far, and was now only 1 metres from the Emperor's palace.

It was dawn. The sun was just beginning to rise over the Colosseum.

Farticus sprinted across a cobbled-stone piazza and hid behind a large statue of Neptune.

Whenever he felt the urge to break wind – which was almost every few minutes – he'd will himself to let out an SBD, a **Silentus But Deadlius**. He couldn't risk popping off some thunderous cracker and drawing attention to himself.

'**PHOOOOSHHHH!**' he let rip. Another SBD. The

pigeons perched on Neptune dropped to the ground like rocks.

'Oops! Sorry, little pigeons,' whispered Farticus. 'I didn't see you there. Fortunately, you're only stunned. You should **snap out of it** once the stench is gone.'

'Farticus!' a voice called out from a dark alley.

Farticus turned to see Cornelius running out of the

shadows into the now sun-soaked piazza.

Farticus smiled. He was overjoyed to see the teenage boy who had helped him and his family flee from the clutches of Bullius all those months ago.

'Wow. It's really you!' Cornelius grinned, through the orange-scented snotus-rag tied across his face. 'I'm glad you dropped that note into my bedroom window yesterday, telling me to meet you here. I bet you're here to save your family!'

'How did you know?' asked Farticus, surprised.

'Everyone in Rome knows that Bullius is holding your family prisoner,' said Cornelius. 'But I also heard. . .'

Cornelius stopped himself.

'Heard what?' pressed Farticus.

'I heard that they are having the time of their lives. Living in the lapus of luxury. Not in a prison cell at all.'

Farticus's thoughts immediately went back to how upset Rhina had been living in Britannia, and for a moment he reflected that she might be better off living this great life with the Emperor. 'But who am I kidding?' he thought. 'I love her and I'm going to save her!' Farticus blurted out.

'That's what I thought you would do,' grinned Cornelius, who was Farticus's number-one fan. 'I can't wait for you to blow them all away! So ... I bet you want to **sneak into the palace somehow**? And I know how you can do it!'

'That's what I wanted to hear,' grinned Farticus, popping off another SBD and knocking the flock of pigeons over again, just as they were coming to.

'So, Druid!' snapped Emperor Bullius, as the soldiers dragged in a man with silver hair and a long, white beard. 'You claim you know a plant that can stop someone from farting?'

'Yes, I do,' mumbled the Druid, who wasn't happy about being man-handled by the soldiers. 'It's actually the yellow flower from the non-ventus plant. Whoever

I have found
the perfect plant to plug
Farticus!

eats it, or drinks a solution of it, won't be able to **let rippus** for several hours.'

'Great! Hand it over!'

As the Druid handed Bullius a sack of non-ventus yellow flowers, General Yesmanus charged into the room, looking extremely flustered.

'Sorry for bursting in like this, your Great One, but Farticus Maximus is in the building!' he panted. 'He snuck in, hidden on a cart with today's delivery of **meat and dead bodies for the lions**.'

'So, the great Farticus has finally arrived! I want everyone, including you, Druid, to gather in the luxury lounging room with his family. And I want a dozen of my best soldiers in there as well. We'll wait for the

A bit over the top!

And where did the cat come from? So cliché!

I'll be rid of Farticus forever! Ha! Ha! Ha! Cackle! Cackle! Ha!

**smelly beast** to make his appearance, and then . . .'

Emperor Bullius flung back his head and let out an evil cackle.

'Goodbye, Farticus. I will **butterfly-kiss** you today,' he snarled under his breath.

# CHAPTERUS NINE

# SURPRISE!

Farticus was running through the long, marbled hallways of the palace.

'Where is everyone?' he wondered. 'There's not even a single soldier around!'

He darted from room to room. Not a soul in sight. He eventually found his way into the luxurious lounging room to find Emperor Bullius draped over a couch and flanked by General Yesmanus, the Druid, and his **entire palace army**. They were all wearing orange-scented snotus-rags. They had clearly been expecting him.

Farticus stopped dead in his tracks. This was a bit of a surprise. And then he caught sight of Rhina, his mother and Rotteneggus standing off to the side.

'Rhina!' he called out.

'Farticus!' she cried, jumping up, only to be pushed back down by one of Bullius's soldiers.

'Let them go, Bullius!' growled Farticus. 'I have eaten enough beans, zucchini, and poorly cooked pig to blow you and your men off the face of this earth. No snotus-rag will save you from what I have been brewing.'

In a flash Farticus whirled around and **pointed his bottomus** in the direction of the soldiers standing closest to him. They **gasped with fright**.

'Put down your bottomus!' pleaded Bullius. 'There's no need for violence. Your family is OK. They have been treated like guests. Isn't that true?'

'Yeah, Dad!' blurted Rotteneggus. 'It's really nice here. And the Emperor said he doesn't want to **butterfly-kiss** you any more. He wants us all to be friends.'

Farticus wasn't sure what to think. He looked at Rhina. She shrugged.

'So nice to see you, son,' added Farticus's mother. 'We really have been treated kindly here. And I believe the Emperor when he says he'd like to make peace with you.'

'Thank you, Helena,' smiled Bullius. 'And to show my kindness to you, dear Farticus, I invite you to come sit with us and **accept some refreshments**. Let's talk this out.'

Emperor Bullius clapped his hands and a troupe of servants breezed in with trays of grapes, cheese and pomegranate juice.

'OK,' stuttered Farticus, still **a little suspicious** of Bullius's friendliness. 'I *am* pretty thirsty. Thank you.'

As Farticus took a swig from the cup filled with juice, Bullius shot a look a meaningful look at the Druid.

Yes! Drink it, loser!

'Ah!' sighed Farticus. 'That was nice! Thanks again.'

'NOW TAKE HIM PRISONER!' Bullius abruptly barked at his soldiers. 'AND PUT HIS FAMILY IN A CAGE. BUT LEAVE THE BOY HERE WITH ME!'

While ten legionnaires rushed to grab hold of Farticus, another troop of soldiers wheeled in a cage and tossed Rhina and Farticus's mother inside it.

'What are you doing!?' panicked Rotteneggus.

'Boy, you have a choice!' said Bullius. 'You can **be my prisoner** or you can be my son and grow up to be a **courageous fighter**.'

Rotteneggus looked at his family, then back at the Emperor.

172

'Don't, son!' pleaded Farticus. 'He doesn't truly love you. Not the way I love you and your brothers.'

Rotteneggus dropped his head, and sidled up next to the Emperor.

'Smart decision, lad,' snorted Bullius.

'I knew it!' huffed Farticus, now wrestling in the grip of Bullius's soldiers. 'I knew this was a trap all along! Now you and your men will pay us for it. Get ready to feel the full force of my **deadly windus**.'

'Go on then!' laughed Bullius, winking at the Druid. 'I'd like to see you try!'

Farticus was confused by Bullius's comment, and his apparent indifference.

'OK, then,' he said. 'Don't say I didn't warn you...'

Farticus screwed up his face and gritted his teeth. From deep within his intestines came a low rumble, a roar, a groan, and finally a **spine-chilling thunderous growl** echoed throughout the chamber.

# BBBRRRRRRRRPPPPPPPPPPP!!!!!!

It was one of the most powerful and potent blasts Farticus had ever unleashed. The soldiers holding on to him were **blown backwards through the air** and tossed up against the wall like rag dolls.

Emperor Bullius shot to his feet – shocked. He turned to the Druid, seething with anger.

'WHAT THE . . . !?? I THOUGHT YOU SAID THE NON-VENTUS PLANT WOULD WORK?' he shouted, now looking a little nervous. 'YOU STUPIDUS WEIRDO MEDICINE MAN FROM BRITANNIA!'

Bullius turned to the remaining soldiers. They had all shuffled to the

back of the room, frightened by Farticus's **deadly cracker of a fart**.

'THROW THE DRUID TO THE LIONS! AND GET FARTICUS!'

'I don't think so!' said the Druid, slowly removing his silver wig and his fake long, white beard.

Emperor Bullius gasped. General Yesmanus gasped. The soldiers gasped. Rhina, Helena and Rotteneggus gasped. But most of all, Farticus gasped.

It was Gassius!

# CHAPTERUS TEN

# A GASSY TWIST

'Gassius!' croaked Farticus. 'I thought, I thought . . .'

'What? That I was dead, kaputus, over and outus, fish foodus?' grinned Gassius.

Farticus nodded.

'Well, it takes more than a sea storm to keep me down . . . oh, and it helped that some dolphins carried me to safety – apparently the smell of **my gas is useless under sea water**. But now I can help you, my friend!'

'WAIT!' screamed Bullius, now shaking in his sandals. 'Why couldn't we smell you? And why didn't you pop off while you were disguised as the Druid?'

'Well, that's because there *is* a non-ventus plant. It's just not the one I gave you,' smirked Gassius. 'I ate the real one, and it stopped me from letting rip for about an hour or so. But that hour is long gone now and I feel some beautiful, **hurricane-like wind brewing** deep in my bottomus... You ready, Farticus?'

'Readier than I'll ever be! Mum, Rhina, Rotteneggus – hit the ground and breathe into your snotus-rags. This isn't going to be pretty!'

Farticus and Gassius swung into ... or should that be, *stunk into* action.

# BBBRRRRRRPPPPPPPP!!!!!!......

# POP! POPPPP! POPPPP!

# BBBRRRRRRRPPPPPPPP!!!!!!......

# BBBRRRRPPPPP!!!!!!......

Bullius's soldiers didn't have a chance to run, as the force of the **smelly gladiators' windus catapulted them** off their feet. The gas was so strong that their armour and helmets were blown clear off their bodies. The legionnaires flew through the air, crashing into each other, choking and spluttering.

Farticus and Gassius had defeated every one of Bullius's men within minutes. They were all out cold.

'Dad!'

Farticus turned to see Bullius clutching Rotteneggus in a headlock and holding a dagger to his throat.

'Put away your bottomus, or the kid gets it!' screamed Bullius, tightening his snotus-rag and gasping between breaths.

'But I thought I was going to be your son?' gulped Rotteneggus.

Bullius tightened his grip.

'Yeah, right!' scoffed Bullius. 'As if I would want a filthy, smelly orphan boy like you to be my son.'

Farticus could see the hurt in Rotteneggus's eyes.

'Let him go, Bullius,' he pleaded.

'Not a chance, **stinkus-head!**' growled Bullius. 'Now listen up. Once my men come to, they will lock you up in a cell. And there will be no resistance or any more popping-off from you two. Otherwise I will **butterfly-kiss** your boy. Got it?'

Farticus glanced over at Gassius. There was nothing they could do.

But suddenly, without any warning, young Rotteneggus let rip a **silentus but deadlius** stinker of a fart.

'Oh, you dirty little . . .' cried Bullius as he raised his hand to his face, **momentarily blinded** by the **rotten cloud** that was too strong even for the orange-scented snotus rag.

Rotteneggus stamped on Bullius's toes and swung his elbow directly into an area of a man where one should never swing an elbow.

'OWWWWW!' groaned Bullius, releasing his grip on Rotteneggus.

Rotteneggus pulled away, only to find himself flat on his face when Bullius grabbed his ankle. Bullius raised the shiny blade of his dagger, ready to plunge it into the back of young Rotteneggus.

'NO!' screamed Rhina. She and Helena had just recovered after being **knocked out** by the stench.

In that moment Farticus leaped toward Bullius and grabbed hold of the dagger. Rotteneggus freed his foot from Bullius's grip and ran to Gassius's side as Farticus and Bullius tumbled on the ground.

And once again Farticus let one rip.

# BBBRRRRRRRPPPPPPPP!!!!!!

Bullius groaned and within moments Farticus had managed to rip the dagger out of his hand and **hug** him deeply in the chest. The **gruesome fight** was over. Bullius was dead.

# CHAPTERUS ELEVEN

# HERO

It wasn't long before the citizens of the Roman Empire learned that their emperor was dead and that they now had a new emperor – Emperor Yesmanus.

Yes, when General Yesmanus came to, after the stinky battle in the palace, and saw Bullius lying lifeless on the tiled floor, he struck a deal with Farticus and Gassius.

HAIL NEW EMPEROR YESMANUS!

'Look, Yesmanus,' said Farticus, 'you allow us to live on our farms just outside of Rome, as free people, and no more gladiator fights for either of us. And we'll back you to be the new emperor. We're still very popular with the *populus*, you know!'

General Yesmanus agreed. (He wasn't called Yesmanus for nothing!)

'I never did like him,' he said. 'Bullius was always a little too crazy for me. And I've always been such a fan of yours, Farticus.'

Everyone was happy with the deal – especially Rhina.

'Oh, Farty, I'm so proud of you,' she said hugging him, thrilled to be back in their villa in the capital. 'Not only are you my hero and the populus's hero, but you're your sons' hero.'

Rhina turned to see Rotteneggus playing with his brothers, who had been brought back from Britannia.

'I'm Farticus Maximus!' Rotteneggus said, holding up a wooden dagger.

'No, I wanna be Dad!' echoed Stinkius and Odorus in unison. 'Long live Farticus Maximus!'

Long live Farticus Maximus!!!